MW01101019

www.veganchildrenbooks.com

 www.facebook.com/veganchildrenbooks

 @veganchildrenbooks

 @veganchildren

 A Pig is a Dog is a Kid &
Milk and Cookie a Little Spooky

For Mateo, whom I love so fiercely,
and for everyone who loves animals.

I created this book because most of you have a natural connection with animals, but few make the connection between our love for animals and the habit of eating them. I offer a closer look at why and how we can so wholeheartedly devote ourselves to certain animals and then allow others to suffer unnecessarily, especially those slaughtered for food. I explain that animals, just like you and me, want to avoid pain and suffering, and I encourage you to think differently about what you choose to eat, always listen to your heart, and show compassion to all living beings.

My first book
Milk and Cookie a Little Spooky
if you didn't have the chance
to read it!

If you enjoyed reading these books,
please leave reviews. Thank you!

www.mascotbooks.com

A Pig is a Dog is a Kid

©2016 Maritza Oliver. All Rights Reserved. No part of this publication may
be reproduced, stored in a retrieval system or transmitted in any form
by any means electronic, mechanical, or photocopying, recording or
otherwise without the permission of the author.

For more information, please contact:
Mascot Books
560 Herndon Parkway #120
Herndon, VA 20170
info@mascotbooks.com

Library of Congress Control Number: 2016910904

CPSIA Code: PRT0916A
ISBN-13: 978-1-63177-907-7

Printed in the United States

A Pig IS a Dog IS a Kid

Why We Treat Animals Differently
and How to Change Our Ways

Written and Illustrated by
Maritza Oliver
Author of *Milk and Cookie a Little Spooky*

We Are a Nation of Animal Lovers!

Your pet sits on your lap, eats out of your hand, and sleeps in your bed. You see him every day and you grow closer as you make memories with him. He's smart and playful. He gives you love and teaches you about friendship, loyalty, and responsibility. He grows up and lives with you as part of your family. You love him and take care of him until the day he dies of old age.

Farmed animals on the other hand...

are forgotten because we do not see them. We've seen an actual pig perhaps once or twice in our lives. They seem quite intelligent based on videos we watch or books we read, but we still don't know much about them.

In general, society sees farmed animals as dumb and of little importance.

We care even less about fish and insects.

We wish we could say...

Pigs are as important to us as dogs, but that would be a lie. If we had dog meat for dinner, we would cover our mouths with our hands to stop ourselves from throwing up, but our mouths water when we think of bacon. Many of us have dogs and cats as pets, and they have a special place in our hearts.

In any case...

We say we love animals, yet we eat cows, pigs, chickens, and turkeys as if these beings are somehow not animals. Is it possible to both love and eat animals?

Don't we ever wonder

how things got this way?

One animal is deserving of our love, while the other only satisfies our appetite. If we truly love animals, then eating meat doesn't really make sense.

Because...

There's **no** way to get meat without killing an animal, and there's **no** way to do that nicely.

We enjoy eating meat and often tend to forget that hotdogs, chicken nuggets, ham, steak, and fish sticks are made from the animals we slaughter.

Now...

Some may say that the animals don't feel anything when they die, they were put here for us to eat, or they are happy to be our food. These people want us to believe these reasons prove that farmed animals are different. They hope these reasons will explain the way they treat these animals. Some might say, "But dogs are meant to be pets, pigs aren't."

If dogs are better as pets, while pigs are raised to be made into bacon, it's because we treat them as such. We treat dogs as friends and minimize the plight of farmed animals. We act like they don't matter.

The Golden Rule says:

"Treat others the way you want to be treated."

Nowhere does it say "unless they're not human."

The point is...

We're all able to love one another, and an important part of love is empathy—being able to understand and share the feelings of others. In other words, we put ourselves in someone else's shoes and feel what they are feeling. Think about...

how you would like to be treated.

Empathy comes so naturally to us.

It can and should spread beyond humans to other living beings and to nature itself.

Besides being empathetic by nature,
we're also compassionate.

The proof is...

If someone was abusing an animal in front of us, we would be outraged. And we would try to stop it if we could. That's because we understand the difference between right and wrong. We should be proud of ourselves for having the courage to step up, be a voice for those whose voices have been ignored, and fight against injustice. That's the real animal rights person in us. The true animal lover!

Until...

Somebody teaches us differently. We should never believe anyone who tells us not to care about the pain and suffering of animals. These are innocent beings who have done nothing wrong to us. If we love animals, we shouldn't try to convince ourselves it's not a big deal to eat their meat.

This just disappoints the animals, and we disappoint ourselves for not doing what is expected of us.

The thing is...

We never think of a pig while eating a BLT (bacon, lettuce, tomato) sandwich, but that "bacon" has two faces.

One is the crispy meat from the sides and belly of a pig with strips of fat. It is salted, smoked, sliced thin, and fried. **The other** is a 350-lb. mammal with hooves, hair, and a "face." Pigs are as intelligent as the dogs who share our homes and even smarter than a three-year-old human child. They are sociable, playful, and curious. They love their families and friends. They build nests, relax in the sun, and cool off in the mud. A pig is more like us than we think. He is someone who will fight for his life to the last breath.

"But we need meat to be healthy. Meat gives us protein and our bodies need protein."

Plant
Power
Plate

FRUITS

VEGETABLES

The truth is we don't need to eat meat to be healthy. In fact, scientists tell us that too much meat can make us unhealthy. Luckily, all foods contain some protein, and if we eat legumes (for example, peas, beans, and lentils), whole grains, nuts, seeds, fruits, and vegetables, we will have everything our body needs to stay healthy!

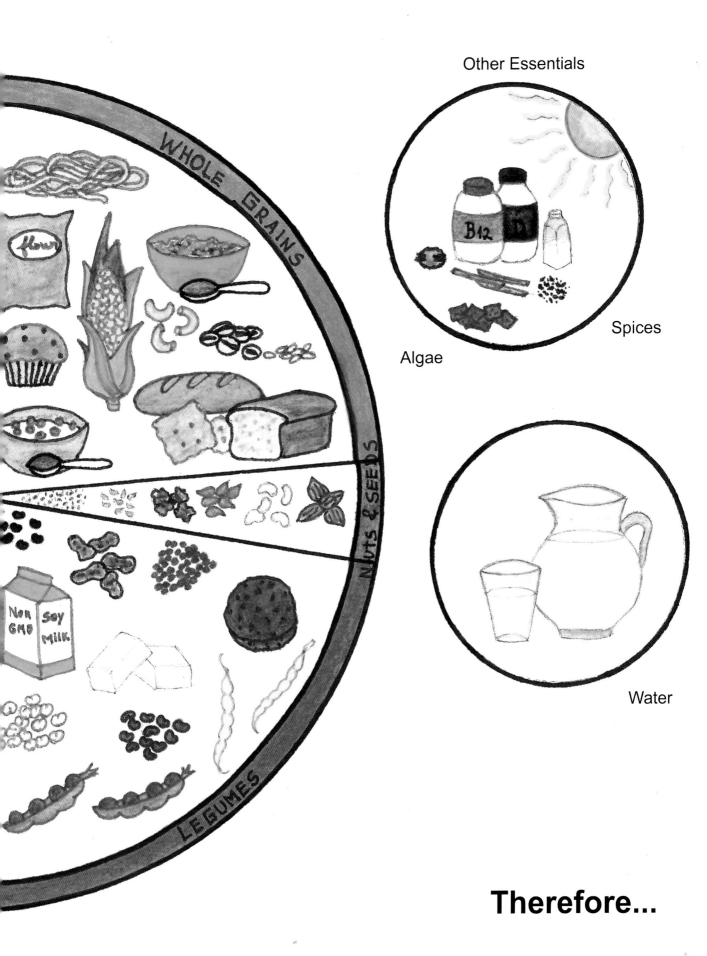

WHOLE GRAINS

Nuts & SEEDS

LEGUMES

Non GMO Soy Milk

flour

Other Essentials

B12

D

Algae

Spices

Water

Therefore...

If we don't need meat, dairy, or eggs to be healthy, it is a choice.

And we can choose not to harm animals who experience pain and pleasure like us. We can choose to put an animal's interest in staying alive before our own desire for their flesh, but we can no longer choose to eat them.

It's not a personal choice when others are harmed.

We've been drawn to animals since we were babies. We've always found them fascinating! We care for them if they share our lives because they make us very happy. Animals are friends, not food. We would rather play with a bunny than eat her, and for good reason! In our hearts we feel we should protect them, and we should always trust this feeling.

Finally...

We must understand we don't eat certain animals because they taste better, or because they're less clever, or because God says it's okay. We eat animals because we're being raised to treat animals this way. We must be smart enough to recognize how our lives are affecting their lives and change for the better.

We are truly a nation of animal lovers!

Let's open our hearts and minds to a way of life that is different from what's being handed down to us. Let's appreciate animals for who they are and focus on what makes us equal instead of what separates us. And if we allow ourselves to get to know these beautiful beings a little bit better, we might fall in love with them a little bit more. We'll then realize that...

In the ability to feel joy and pain, we are all the same.
When it comes to suffering, a pig is a dog is a kid.

Author's Note:

There is an important group that fights for animals to be treated fairly. This group is known as the "Vegan Movement" and continues to grow as more people understand that animals need to be treated with kindness. People are fighting and risking their lives to save animals all over the world because we finally realized that humans won't be able to survive on this planet without animals.

And just because you feel you can't do much, it doesn't mean you shouldn't do anything.

So what can one small individual like you do?

First, remember that knowledge is power! There is a lot of information out there that can be easily found on YouTube, Google, and in the books at your public library. Read widely. Spend a month studying animal cruelty on the internet. You will find some disturbing images and videos, but they are truthful.

Second, ask your parents to find the vegan community in your city. You'll be surprised at how many we are! Spread the message of kindness to animals everywhere you go, wear a T-shirt with this message, visit your local animal sanctuaries, take part in public demonstrations, volunteer with animal rights groups, teach your friends and family to care for animals, and fight for animals to be treated fairly. Believe in yourself and in what you stand for, and don't let anything hold you back.

Lastly, for every person who asks why you don't eat farmed animals anymore, this book explains it in detail. Just share this book with them, or send them a copy as a gift!

Thank you for making the world a better place. The future is bright.

Vegan Love,

Maritza Oliver